# Book No. 1

# Gladys the Dragon
# and
# The Lost Lamb

### Written by
### Elsie Bell

### Illustrated by
### Ray Schofield

Gladys the Dragon Series
edited by
Roger Wickham

**Pond View Books**

# About these stories

Gladys is a sleepy, friendly dragon who doesn't fly any more. She will tell you she has 'quite given it up'. But in her dreams she **does** fly, and in some of her adventures she flies off to a castle of long ago where a young girl called Lady Gwendolyn lives.

However, in this first book, we find out how Gladys got her name and how she helped the farm children's pet lamb.

The dragon's best friend is George, an eight year old boy who lives near the farm where Gladys has made her home in a small cave on a rocky hillside.

Gladys has many more adventures.

I hope you enjoy them all.

Elsie Bell.

This is where Gladys and George live.

# The Lost Lamb

There was the dragon, strolling through the fields enjoying the lovely day. She was humming a little tune to herself and feeling very sleepy. Of course, dragons of long ago FLEW about everywhere, but this one was rather lazy. Except in her dreams, she never flew anywhere.

She lay down in the long grass, rolled over, and felt the sun warming her tummy. A daisy tickled her nose, and she blew it gently away. Even though she was sleepy, she had more sense than to blow too hard. Because you know what happens when dragons blow too hard, don't you?

One of her friends was a boy called George, and they often sat down in the grass together for a chat. George and his dog Kerry were looking for the dragon, but they couldn't see her anywhere.

Dragons are a beautiful shade of green, and so like the colour of grass that nobody could see her as she snoozed happily in the afternoon sun.

The dragon lies down in the long grass.

But Kerry the dog soon found the sleepy dragon and woke her up by licking her on the nose.

"That's enough Kerry," laughed George, "she's awake now."

"Kerry is a nice name," yawned the dragon, "I wish I had a name, I'm fed up with only being known as 'the dragon'. How would you like it George if you were just known as 'the boy'? And Kerry wouldn't like to be called 'the dog', would he?"

"Hmm." George was thoughtful for a moment. "I suppose you really should have a name. Are you sure you haven't got one?"

"Well, if I have, no-one ever told me what it is," the dragon replied sadly.

George suggested the name Alice. He had an Auntie Alice he was very fond of, but the dragon wasn't keen on the name. Then George made lots of suggestions, like Barbara, Claribel, Dora, Eunice, Genevieve, Mavis, Olive, Petronella, Selina, and Winifred. But the dragon didn't seem to care for any of them.

The dragon wants a name.

The next day, the dragon was having a lovely sleep in the warm grass, and Kerry the dog was racing about in the wood, leaping over streams and getting lots of exciting scents.

George had climbed a tree to try and get a better view, but there was no sign of either of them.

The dragon was wakened by children's voices. It was the farm children, Ella, Katy, and young Johnny, and they were calling, "Gladys, Gladys, where have you gone?" They sounded worried and were searching everywhere.

The dragon could see a very small lamb all by itself in the long grass. The lamb seemed to get tired suddenly, and lay down to sleep just as the sun went behind the clouds.

The children's voices were getting further and further away, and the sleeping lamb began to shiver in the cool air.

The baby lamb is lost and cold.

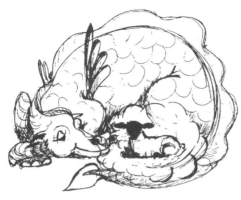

Such a tiny creature needed to be kept warm. It was a pet lamb and had to be fed with a bottle at the farmhouse.

The dragon went over to where the baby lamb was huddled, and lay down beside it. Then an extraordinary thing happened. The dragon took a few low, r-r-rumbly breaths and blew gently on the lamb to warm it up.

When dragons do their special r-r-rumbly breathing, it is very warm and cosy. The lamb soon stopped shivering and slept on quite peacefully.

The dragon headed for the wood to look for George. She was sure that **he** would know what to do with the lamb.

But when she reached the trees and looked back over her shoulder to the field, she saw something brown with a furry tail slinking through the grass towards the lamb.

## It was a hungry fox.

The fox creeps up to the baby lamb.

Although George was still up the tree, he hadn't been able to see Kerry, but Kerry had found George.

The dog was wagging his tail at the bottom of the tree, and George was very pleased to see him.

George had just spotted the sleeping lamb, and the hungry fox getting ready to pounce.

"Quick Kerry, off you go boy," called George, and the dog scampered out of the wood as fast as his little legs would carry him. He barked his special **fierce** bark and chased the fox all the way out of the field.

"Good boy, well done Kerry," said George, when the little dog returned looking very pleased with himself.

The dog chases the fox from the field.

 Meanwhile, the lamb had woken and stood up on her wobbly legs, but she was safe now, and soon the dragon heard the children's voices again.

The children came closer and closer, until Ella called out happily, "I've found Gladys."

The other children came running over, picked up the lamb and began to stroke her, saying, "Thank goodness we've found you."

Little Johnny said, "Where have you been you naughty girl?" He had often heard his mum say that to his sisters.

And off they went towards the farmhouse to give the baby lamb a bottle of her favourite milk.

14

The baby lamb is safe again.

 When George came out of the wood, he told the dragon how he had seen the fox and sent Kerry to the rescue.

And the dragon told him all about how the lamb had been lost and cold and that, if it hadn't been for Kerry's fantastic bravery, the lamb would have been taken away by the hungry fox.

"The lamb is called Gladys," she told him. "I heard the children calling her name."

That night when she was snuggled up in her cosy cave in the hillside, the dragon dreamt about the lamb and the fox, and the children calling, "Gladys, Gladys, where have you gone?"

She woke up thinking that Gladys was a splendid name.

"That's the name for me," she decided.

The dragon chooses her name.

The next day was a Saturday, and George and his dad were having a bonfire in the field when the dragon came along. She said she had something very exciting to tell them.

"I've decided on my name at last. It's **Gladys**, just like the lamb."

George was delighted, and his dad said, "How do you do, Gladys?"

Then George got out some marshmallows and started arranging them on a fallen tree.

"There you are," he declared proudly. And there, spelt out carefully with marshmallows, was the dragon's new name

# GLADYS

How do you do, Gladys?

While they were all admiring George's handiwork, the fire nearly went out. Gladys had to quickly do a few of her special r-r-rumbly breaths to get it going again.

They were all so busy with the fire that when they looked back at the fallen tree, they were surprised to see that all the marshmallows had gone.

Completely disappeared, every single one of them! **Where had they gone?**

Then they noticed that the little dog Kerry was licking his lips and looking rather pleased with himself.

"You little scamp," laughed George's dad, "but I suppose you deserve a reward for saving the baby lamb yesterday."

"Anyway," said George, "Gladys prefers her marshmallows toasted."

Gladys does a few r-r-rumbly breaths.

What a lovely afternoon they all had.

They toasted bread and sausages on the end of sticks, and then they did the same with the rest of the marshmallows.

Kerry had a fine time too. He followed everyone about and ate all the tasty bits that fell off their sticks.

And the dragon had such a full tummy that she was soon fast asleep, dreaming happily about toasted marshmallows, the baby lamb from the farm, and a very special dragon called Gladys.

THE END

Gladys enjoys her picnic by the fire.

## TITLES AVAILABLE NOW

| | | |
|---|---|---|
| 1. | Gladys the Dragon and The Lost Lamb | 1 871044 65 0 |
| 2. | Gladys the Dragon in Gladys Saves the Day | 1 871044 66 9 |
| 3. | Gladys the Dragon and The Flying Lesson | 1 871044 67 7 |
| 4. | Gladys the Dragon and The Slippery Slope | 1 871044 68 5 |
| 5. | Gladys the Dragon meets Lady Gwendolyn | 1 871044 69 3 |
| 6. | Gladys the Dragon and The Mountain Bike | 1 871044 70 7 |

More titles available Summer 1998

Order copies from your usual bookseller